This book belongs to

_____

WALT DISNEY

VOLUME
11

WELCOME BACK, SNOW WHITE

WELCOME BACK

WALT DISNEY FUN-TO-READ LIBRARY

Welcome Back, Snow White All rights reserved. Copyright © MCMLXXXVI The Walt Disney Company.
This book may not be reproduced, in whole or in part, by mimeograph or any other means.
ISBN 1-885222-23-8
Advance Publishers Inc., P.O. Box 2607, Winter Park, FL. 32790
Printed in the United States of America
09876543

One day, a man on a horse rode up to the house where the Seven Dwarfs lived.

"A letter from the castle for the Seven Dwarfs," he said.

"I wonder if this is from Snow White!" said Doc. "Why, it is! And she is coming to see us." Doc went inside to tell the rest of the dwarfs the news.

"Hurray!" shouted the dwarfs. They jumped for joy.

"How wonderful!" cried Happy.
"I have missed Snow White very much,"
said Bashful.

"Yes," said Grumpy. "It is wonderful news. But what will Snow White think when she sees our house?"

The sink was full of dirty dishes.
The chairs were broken.
There was dust everywhere.

Dirty clothes lay on the floor.

Old shoes lay all about.

The curtains had holes in them. And they were gray with dust.

"*A-a-achoo!*" sneezed Sneezy. "There is a lot of dust in here!"

"Well, we will just have to clean it up," said Doc. "Come on."

Doc marched to the sink. He washed all of the dirty dishes.

"There!" he said happily. All the dishes were clean. He left them next to the sink to dry. And off he went to find something else to clean.

Sleepy looked around for something to do. He saw the dishes beside the sink.

Carefully, he put them back into the sink.

"There," he yawned. "Now they can soak for a while. I'll just go take a nap until they are clean."

Dopey swept all the dust into one big pile. But he did not know what to do with it. He went off to find Doc. Doc would know what Dopey should do next.

Sneezy walked by. The great pile of dust tickled his nose.

"*A-a-achoo!*" he sneezed. It was a very big sneeze. Dust blew all over the cottage. It blew all over Sneezy too.

Next came Grumpy. The dust blew in his eyes. His pail of soap and water spilled all over the floor!

Just then Happy walked across the wet floor.

With a *whoosh*, Happy fell down. He tried to stand. But he could not. Instead he slid across the floor.

Sleepy woke up from his nap. He had forgotten all about the dishes. He blinked his eyes. He yawned and stretched.

He started to make up the beds. But he
didn't even finish one bed. He said, "Ho-hum.
I think I'll take another nap." And quick as a
wink, Sleepy fell fast asleep.

"A fine job of cleaning up we've done," said Grumpy.

"The place does look worse than when we started," Doc agreed sadly.

"The trouble is, we are not working together," said Doc. "Let's decide who is going to do what."

"Then we can all help each other," said Happy.

Doc gave each of the dwarfs a job to do. Sneezy washed the clothes.

Dopey put the wet clothes on the
line to dry.

"It's easier to clean when someone
helps you," said Sneezy.

Doc took out a pail of glue. He glued
new bottoms to the dwarfs' old shoes.

Bashful sat in a corner nearby. He brushed the shoes that Doc had mended. He brushed and brushed. At last they were shiny and clean. Then he lined them up neatly, all in a row.

Grumpy began to mend the broken chairs. He hammered so loud that he woke up Sleepy.

"Well, it's about time you came down to help," grumbled Grumpy.

"Sleepy, you clean the table while I mend the chairs," said Grumpy.

With a big clean cloth, Sleepy washed the table.

"*Humph!*" said Grumpy. "This table looks pretty good!"

Happy was busy making a cake.
Dopey liked watching Happy bake.
When Happy was through, Dopey licked
the spoon clean!

After the cake was done, all the dwarfs gathered around.

"Great job!" said Doc.

"It smells so good," said Sleepy. "I guess my next nap can wait!"

"All right, everyone. Snow White will be here soon. We must get to work. To the table—quick!"

Dopey looked out the door. Sleepy looked
out the window. They were waiting to greet
Snow White.

"Hurry, everyone," said Doc. "We must all wash up!"

"Wash up?" grumbled Grumpy.

"Yes," said Doc.

Quickly everyone lined up to wash.
Finally they all looked neat and clean.
Except for Bashful. He was nowhere to
be found.

"Well look who's here!" said Happy.
There stood Bashful. He was holding a big bunch of flowers.
"I picked these for Snow White," he said.

Just then the dwarfs heard the sound of a carriage.

"She is here! She is here!" they shouted.

All the dwarfs ran outside. Even Bashful
came and stood shyly behind Doc. Everyone
waited for the carriage to stop. Out of the
carriage stepped the beautiful Snow White.

"Welcome back, Snow White," sang the Seven Dwarfs.

Snow White looked just like a princess. Her sweet smile, her gentle hands, and the love in her eyes were the same as ever.

"Oh, I am so happy to see you all!" said Snow White.

"It is good to be back." She kissed Dopey. His eyes lit up. She kissed Grumpy. His face got all red.

And she gave Bashful a special hug.

Then Snow White went inside the cottage.
"Oh, my goodness!" she said. "Everything
is so neat and sparkling clean!"

"We wanted it to be just right for you," said Grumpy.

"And Doc showed us how to work together," said Happy.

"Well you should all be very proud of yourselves," she said. "I am glad you have learned to work together so very well!"

The dwarfs poked each other. They blushed with pride.

"Working together makes the work easier!" they all agreed. Then they laughed and told stories for the rest of the day.